T0193502

Attack of the Wolves

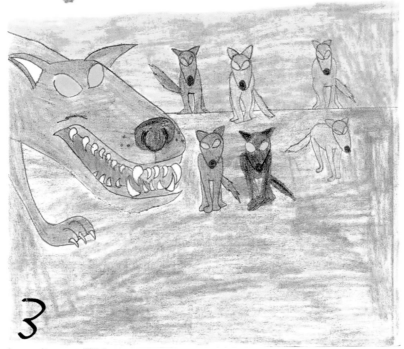

3

Attack of the wolves
A LION CUB'S ADVENTURES SEASON 1, EPISODE 3:

Copyright © 2020 Liam Frew.

iUniverse books may be ordered through booksellers or by contacting:

iUniverse
1663 Liberty Drive
Bloomington, IN 47403
www.iuniverse.com
844-349-9409

Because of the dynamic nature of the Internet, any web addresses or links contained in this book may have changed since publication and may no longer be valid. The views expressed in this work are solely those of the author and do not necessarily reflect the views of the publisher, and the publisher hereby disclaims any responsibility for them.

Any people depicted in stock imagery provided by Getty Images are models, and such images are being used for illustrative purposes only.
Certain stock imagery © Getty Images.

ISBN: 978-1-6632-1248-1 (sc)
ISBN: 978-1-6632-1249-8 (e)

Library of Congress Control Number: 2020921444

Print information available on the last page.

iUniverse rev. date: 10/30/2020

table of contents

chapter 1. a domestic crime

It all started at night at a village...all villagers were asleep, no noise was out, and the dog was on patrol

at the sheep pen

2 minutes later... after the sleeping villagers heard noises outside of their huts
what was that?
Something was after the sheep!
bark! bark!
2 animals got into the pen and killed 5 of the sheep and dragged 2 of them away
wheres the two sheep?
two sheep are missing!

Chapter 2. out and attacked

next morning...Lion cub and raccoon were out for a walk...

but...they don't know... that they're being watched

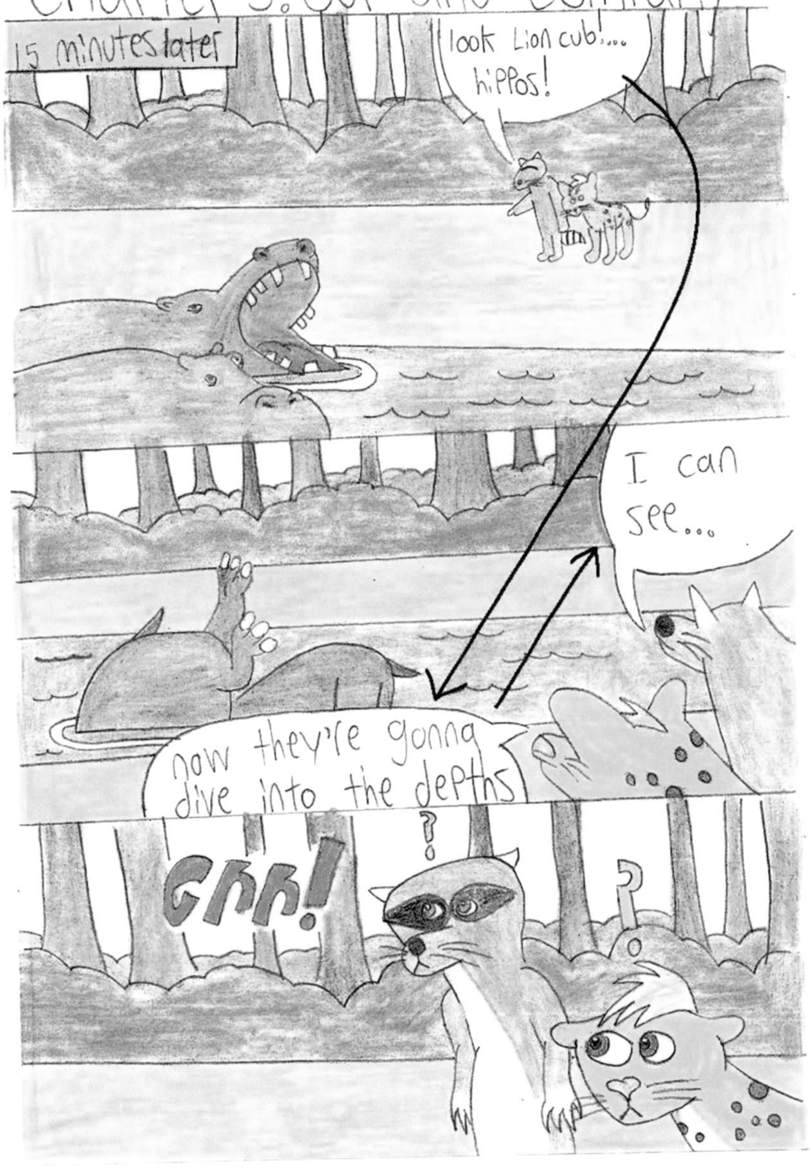

Chapter 6. return of the wolves

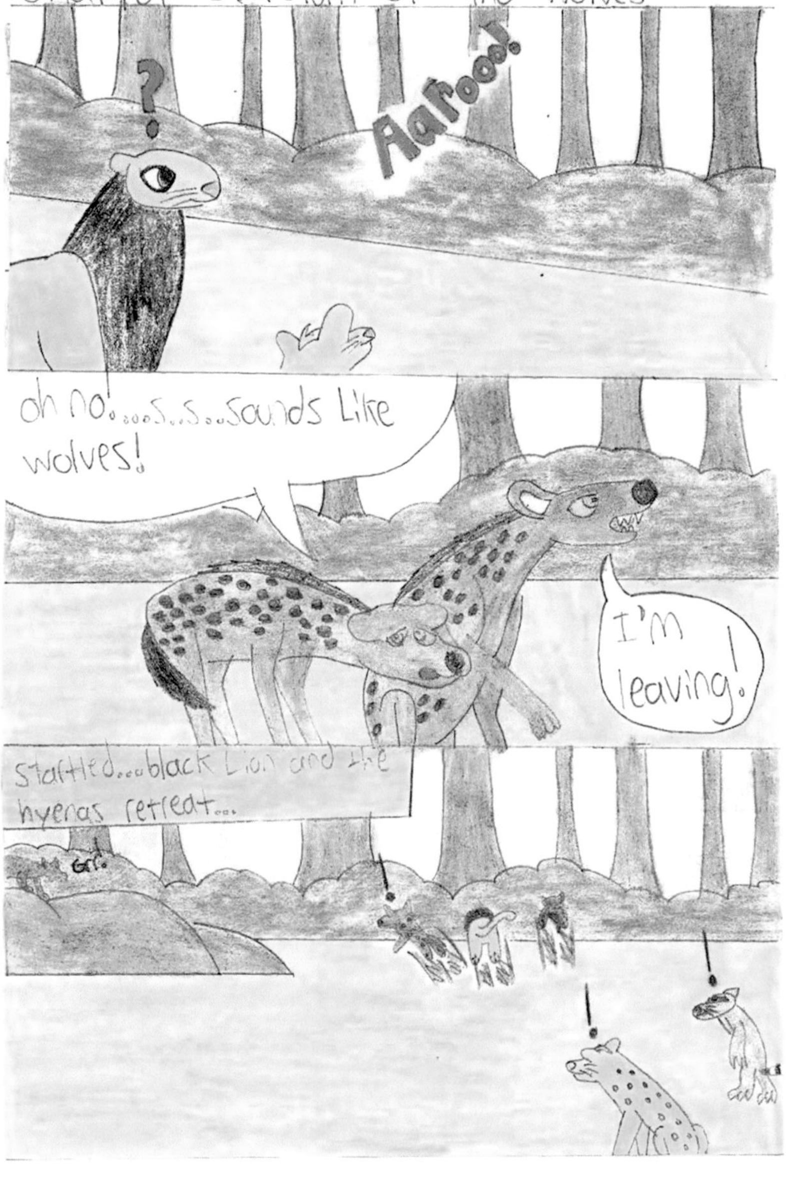

Printed in the United States
By Bookmasters